The Bees
Down in the Garden

By DC Swain
Illustrated by Anna Bonita

Written by DC Swain
Illustrated by Anna Bonita
Published by Cambridge Town Press
(C) 2015 DC Swain
All Rights Reserved.
ISBN 978-0-473-39423-3
dcswain.com

For Caitlin.

Down in the garden
beyond the apple trees,
is a fading blue hive
full of busy bees.

Basking in the warmth
of mid-morning sun,
the hive is alive with a
great buzzing hum.

With a stretch of the legs
and a flutter of wings,
the bees set out to do
all manner of things.

Flying up high
in the clear morning air,
the search for fun and mischief
wherever they dare.

They flit through the orchard
of bulging fruit trees,
stopping for a taste
of whatever they please.

Back near the hive
a big dog has strayed,
they let out a "Buzz!"
and scare it away.

An excited hum
the hive has been saved,
a quick snack of nectar
and they're back on their way.

Finally they get to
the work of the day,
collecting up pollen
wherever they may.

From sweet smelling flowers
they take to the air,
back to the hive
their honey-making lair.

At the end of the day
in fading sunlight
they return to the hive
and wish each other "Goodnight".

The End

CPSIA information can be obtained
at www.ICGtesting.com
Printed in the USA
BVHW021329150620
581241BV00034B/335